Gampy's Lamps

by Lee S. Justice
illustrated by Alexandra Wallner

 HOUGHTON MIFFLIN   BOSTON

On the first day of spring, the outdoor flea market opened. Gampy and I wandered from table to table. I had already bought a toy. Gampy was still looking. I knew what he was looking for.

Gampy's eyes lit up. "I think I see my prize, Brenda," he whispered to me. He pointed to a glass container. Its handle had the shape of an ear. I picked it up and ran my finger over the glass. "Is it a kerosene lamp?" I asked.

"Yes, indeed," Gampy said.

When we came home, my mother rolled her eyes. "Not more junk!" she said.

"I have a real prize this time!" declared Gampy, holding up his lamp. "I paid only four dollars for it!"

My mother groaned in a joking way. "Don't you have that one already?"

"Not *exactly* like this one," Gampy answered. Then he chuckled. "At least, I don't think they're the same," he added.

Gampy was my mother's grandfather and my great-grandfather. Gampy collected old lamps. He found them at flea markets, yard sales, thrift shops, and other places like those.

My mother believed the lamps were useless. They had no electric wires and no holder for a light bulb. Most of the lamps were made before houses had electricity. Back then, there were no battery-powered flashlights or electric lights. These lamps held oil, usually kerosene. To use it, the burner in the lamp was lit. As the oil burned, the lamps gave light.

I learned about oil lamps from Gampy. He began collecting them as a hobby after he retired from his job. A few years later, my mother said that our small apartment was getting too cluttered. Gampy's lamp collection would have to go. So Gampy moved all the lamps to a storage room in the basement of our building.

I rode the elevator down to the storage room with Gampy. He unlocked the door and flicked on the light switch. We entered the little room.

Lamps and parts of lamps filled the shelves against one wall. Clear glass chimneys stood in a row. Some lamps were short and round. Others were tall and graceful. Most of the lamps were clear glass. Some were tin. Some lamps had decorations. Boxes on the floor held lamp parts for Gampy to use for mending his lamps.

The lamps belonged to people who lived long ago. I liked to think about that. I imagined a girl my age, but living more than one hundred years before I was born. Every night, the girl picked up one of the little glass hand lamps. Its flame showed her the way to her bedroom. She placed the lamp on a table, and it glowed as she got into bed. The oil quickly burned up, and the lamp went out.

Gampy set his new prize next to a lamp that looked just like it. He stood there smiling as he watched them.

"Which one should we talk about today?" Gampy asked me. I reached for a lamp with a handle and a curved shape.

"This one looks like it could have belonged to the boy named Aladdin," Gampy said. "You know who Aladdin was, don't you?" he asked me.

"I saw the movie," I answered.

"The movie?" Gampy raised his eyebrows. "I don't mean that cartoon guy," he said. "I mean the Aladdin in the famous old fairy tale."

Gampy talked about the poor boy named Aladdin who found an oil lamp in an enchanted underground garden. Aladdin discovered by accident that a genie would appear when the lamp was rubbed. The genie would grant any wish. Aladdin used the wonderful lamp to become rich. He built a palace decorated with sparkling jewels, and he married the lovely daughter of a king.

When Gampy finished the tale, I rubbed the lamp hard and pretended to be making a wish. Gampy laughed. Then he took a lamp from the shelf and pointed to something written on the brass part. "What do you see on this burner?" Gampy asked me.

I looked closely. "Aladdin!" I read.

"Yes, indeed. Now, why might a lamp company choose that name?" Gampy asked with a wink.

Sometimes Gampy told me tales like the one about Aladdin. Sometimes he told me true stories.

"I grew up in the country," Gampy said. "Electric power had been around for more than thirty years. But there were still no electric lines on our road. Electricity cost too much for most folks, anyway. We cooked on a wood-burning stove. We got warmth from the stove and from fireplaces. And we lit our rooms with oil lamps." Gampy gazed at the lamp in his hands. "Just like this one."

I went to bed that night, picturing Gampy as a boy my age reading by his oil lamp.

The next morning, I awoke with a strange feeling. The clock said ten past four. But sunlight was already filling the room. I listened for the usual morning sounds. I heard no TV. I heard no beeping of the microwave oven. No humming of the refrigerator. No traffic outside. There was only silence.

I hurried to the window, and what I saw amazed me. The street and sidewalks were completely coated with ice. Thick icicles were draped over the edges of rooftops. The parked cars looked like giant shiny ice cubes. No cars were driving on the slick street. Everything gleamed and sparkled.

"Last night's rain turned into ice," my mother explained. "The ice storm knocked out the power lines, so we have no electricity." She was listening through her headset to a radio report. "No school today," she said. "People should not try to drive. The whole city has no power."

We spent the morning indoors. I realized how many things in our house ran on electricity, because nothing seemed to work. My mother and Gampy couldn't have their morning coffee because the coffeemaker didn't work. The stove didn't work. We couldn't use the microwave oven, the toaster, or the dishwasher. My mother worried about the food spoiling in the refrigerator. I couldn't play games on the computer. I couldn't watch TV. We had no hot water or heat.

I read a book. My mother and I put together part of a jigsaw puzzle. I talked on the phone with my friend. Then I just stared out the window and watched the dripping icicles.

By the afternoon, the sun had melted most of the ice. "Let's get some fresh air, Brenda," my mother suggested, and we went outside.

14

Everyone else must have had the same idea. Neighbors were strolling and chatting and meeting one another for the first time. People had brought chairs outside and were playing checkers and chess and other games. A few people had set up barbecues and offered to grill food. The neighborhood felt so friendly and lively.

The sun set. The sky turned gray, then black. The street was as dark as a closet. Gampy brought out several lanterns. He filled them with kerosene and set them up at the entrance to our building. He lit them. They glowed with a welcoming light.

"Have you got any more of those to lend?" asked a man who lived across the street.

"Yes, indeed," said Gampy. He carried one of the lanterns inside so that he could find his way to the storage room. When he came out, he had a box full of lamps. More neighbors came by to borrow them.

The power did not come on for another two days. I was glad when we had electricity again. But I was also glad that I had something beautiful to remember. I would never forget how the night was aglow with the soft, golden lights of Gampy's lamps.

Responding

Think About the Selection

1 What are Gampy's lamps?

2 Why do you think Gampy enjoys collecting these lamps?

3 Do Brenda and her mother feel the same way about Gampy's lamps? Tell why or why not.

4 Do you think you would have liked living in a time before there was electricity? Tell why or why not.

Making Connections This story tells how Gampy's lamps became special for other people too. Have you read another story about a character who shares something that is special to him or her with other people? How are these stories alike? How are they different? Create drawings of the things that are special and tell how they were shared with other people.

ISBN 0-618-29222-5

9 780618 292226

3.6.2

HOUGHTON MIFFLIN

1-51666